Perfect and Other Stories
Femdom Mind Control
Flash Fiction – Vol. 38

S.B.

Disclaimer

This is a work of fiction. Names, characters, business, events, and incidents are the products of the author's imagination. Any resemblance to actual persons, living or dead, or actual events is purely coincidental. All characters are over 18.

Table of Contents

There's nothing better than giving in.

Thank you to all patrons of Spell... B-O-U-N-D.

Afraid of Himself

Andrew Wells was afraid. Not of what was happening around him or whatever crisis the world could throw his way that Friday morning, but of himself, and all the things he was considering doing to prove his worth in the eyes of a Nubian Goddess he had never met for real.

Her name was Mikayla Sommers, her title Empress, and her game, the art of hypnotic femdom. A skilled Hypnodomme with hundreds of entranced minds at her beck and call scattered around the world, she had built the reputation of being one of the most erotically charged women in existence, a soul capable of bending others to her will in the most devious ways imaginable. No warnings of how dangerous she really was, did her justice. To enter her realm was to entertain the possibility of becoming another one of her drones.

Andrew didn't want that at first. He wasn't sure he even wanted to be in the chatroom he found himself in three months prior. A stroke of curiosity had him wander the Internet until he got lost, and once there, finding his way back had proven impossible. Like a moth to a flame, he approached Mikayla wondering what it would be like to lose his mind once, and the first thing she said to him in reply was,

"There's no such thing as 'once'. The rabbit hole is deeper than you think, and it never really ends."

"Rabbit hole?" he remembered asking although many other details of the conversation were nothing short of a blur.

"Yes, like in Alice in Wonderland. It's a common metaphor for trance. Once you start falling, the drop is intense, and your perspective changes whether you want it or not. To take on such a journey with me is to cherish the fact that the hole will grow bigger all the time and that your thoughts will go deeper in the same measure. You will be taken and reshaped to fit the idea I design for you, all consensual, of course. If this is not something you sincerely crave, then you should leave this chatroom and not come back because if I become interested in you, you'll want that interest to never wane. What do you say? Can you handle me inside your head?"

He didn't know for sure, but he believed he did. Whether that conclusion came from pride or something else was a mystery as big as her. The experiences Mikayla promised were new and exciting, wonderful opportunities to get away from increasingly boring routines and ideas that no longer benefitted him. Why not play with an Empress and see where that went? Andrew accepted her offer and signed the contract of his entrancement in both blood and cum.

Ninety-one days later, he sat in bed, looking at the alarm clock and feeling completely out of himself. Empress deserved gifts and monetary tributes every waking hour. As her toy, it was his duty to provide. What he made from his day job barely covered the monthly expenses, let alone the costs of pampering the superior woman who owned him, so he had to find alternatives, and he had to do it fast. Getting another job was one, but the economy wasn't on his side. He didn't have that many valuables worth selling except his body and he didn't want to down there just yet. The only other option that came to mind was...

"Yes, that could work," he thought, his mind drifting in a sea of errors and not really connected to the rest of his body. "I'll make you proud, my Empress. Just wait and see." He was still afraid, yet it was time to face the music. and dance to oblivion.

Andrew got dressed, had a quick breakfast, and then left the house in a hurry, a firearm concealed in the inner pocket of his leather jacket. The nearest bank was about to open.

Glory to Harukka!

Something hard and sticky rammed Yasmin's ass repeatedly, making her dark brown eyes roll to the back of her head. The Latina junior attorney that had recently moved to California to pursue her ambitions in the world of criminal law was chained by a brick wall, partially suspended in the air while her body served as a guinea pig to an insidious plan. The object assailing her was a jumbo-sized dildo though, in her slightly feverish mind, she imagined a green tentacle of some Lovecraftian-inspired horror destined to doom humanity to eternal madness. If she wasn't there already, it wouldn't take long now.

Distorted voices were all around her, emanating from the same abominations that had trapped her on the sub-floor of her workplace, Hartwell & Sons. Three of them had masculine traits while the other two were more feminine. The latter appeared to be in charge, barking their grievances to the male underlings.

"Why did you bring her down here? This wasn't supposed to happen!" A tall redhead said.

"She saw too much," said a bald man. "Once she's reprogrammed, she'll no longer be a threat to our plans."

"She was going to be reprogrammed in due time, idiot!" the other woman exclaimed. "Or do you think we leave the company's hiring policies to chance? Her name has been on the list to join our cause since she was born. You know who her mother was!"

"I'm sorry, Gaia," the bald man continued, "but when we saw her snooping around, we..."

"You panicked, that's what, because that's what morons do instead of keeping their emotions in check. And stop using my real name! The title is all you need."

"Yes, Goddess. Anything you say, Goddess," he crawled to kiss her booted feet, receiving only a kick in his engorged balls in return. "It's too late to stop the process now though."

"I guess so, but you're still going to pay for your transgressions. All of you are. Report to Floor 2 for a prolonged session in the rewiring chamber."

"Goddess? Please don't..."

"That's an order, slave! Go now before I add a day to your sentence every time you open your mouth."

The bald man gulped and so did his companions, but Yasmin couldn't see any of this, only picture their humiliation in her frail mind. She imagined three giant slugs dragging themselves across the basement floor, completely defeated. They would always be at the bottom of the food chain, squished by their superiors, for they deserved nothing more.

When the three men left, the remaining players approached her naked body, assuming equidistant positions to the left and right of her sweaty butt cheeks. The one that had been referred to as Gaia spoke first,

"I'm sorry this is happening this way, sister, but now you have to endure it. The breaking process is usually swift, but necessary to ensure your permanent loyalty to the company. When it's done, you'll be branded like the rest of us and then you'll be initiated into the mysteries that determine our way of life. You never had an actual choice in the matter, so rejoice with that knowledge. You belong to Harukka. You will obey Her!"

"Glory to Harukka!" said the other woman, and Yasmin surprised herself by repeating the same sentence with a stupid smile on her lips. She remembered the name of the ancient demon from the horror stories her mother used to tell her when she was a child, and now the stories had become true.

The dildo/tentacle continued to destroy her ass as her mind succumbed to the first layers of forced indoctrination. Her destiny had already been written: to be the slut acolyte of a higher power. Glory to Harukka now and forever!

It's My Turn Again

The chess game was going far longer than normal, which surprised Alan greatly. Melissa had never been much of a player, always falling for the most basic of traps, and yet here she was, pulling out tricks that would confuse even the most experienced champions with incredible ease. How she was doing this well so suddenly was a mystery waiting to be solved.

"Have you been taking lessons from a Master or something?" he asked, stopping the clock momentarily to gaze into her cerulean eyes.

"I thought we weren't supposed to talk while playing," she replied, crossing her tanned legs under the wood table. She was rocking a leather mini-skirt that day that was a match for her auburn hair. A provocative low-cut, black top completed the attire, but he was smart enough not to get distracted by her juicy boobs.

"And you weren't supposed to be this good. How are you doing this?"

"I got better," she smirked dismissively.

"Too quickly for my taste and anyone else that knows the intricacies of the game. Even if you're taking lessons, it's unlikely you learned so much since the last time we played, unless..."

"Unless what?"

"Unless you have someone whispering the right moves in your ear right now."

"Are you accusing me of cheating?"

"I'm merely raising a hypothesis," he scratched his chin. "Wireless earbuds, perhaps? Although that would be quite the cheap trick."

Melissa stretched in her seat and parted the flowing hair from her narrow ears. "Not as cheap as your innuendo," she said. "Nothing in here, as you can see. Care to apologize now?"

"No. Not until I get a definitive answer. It took me years to get to the level where I am and you're undoing it in a matter of weeks, so I ask once again: how are you doing this?"

"Why are you asking me something you already know?"

"Huh?"

"You're wasting precious time with questions you don't really want an answer to. Not one spoken out loud, of course."

"What are you talking about?" he queried, visibly baffled.

"Think for a moment who the best person to defeat you is and then we can talk. Until then, my mouth is shut."

Alan fumed on the inside. Melissa had always loved her riddles even they were kids, but she had become more exasperating after her twenties. When she wanted to deflect a conversation, it was almost impossible to stop her and not merely because of her lovely body. Her mind was sharper than the rest of her friends, and he feared for the anatomy of anyone who dared to call her an air-headed bimbo. He looked at the board, reviewing all the moves that it had taken to reach the present configuration when the strangest thing came to mind. Not once did he actually remember seeing her move a piece.

"Wait a minute," he thought, a fog unlike any other clouding his better judgment. Playing black, her countermoves matched the ones he would have made if he were in her shoes and if she hadn't touched the pieces at all, then...

"It's my turn again," she whispered, four simple words that triggered an automatic response. Alan's right hand inched forward to reach for the Queen, the most powerful piece in the game, but not as irresistible as her. The suggestion worked once again, binding him deeper to her hypnotic control. He blinked as he let go of the piece, now resting in a perfect place to launch an all-out offensive against his remaining defenses.

"I..." he mumbled. "You..."

"... can't resist," she completed, a truth well-known despite hardly being remembered. He could play for the two of them while she played with his mind. "Happy now, Alan?"

His cock pushed hard against the tight pants, barely holding itself together. Alan bit his lower lip as the ecstasy of surrendering turned his perception of reality into whatever she wanted it to be.

"Anything else you want to ask?"

He didn't offer a response, too busy forgetting he had even asked a thing. The game continued until its obvious conclusion, with a wannabe king wrapped between her legs. The winner takes it all.

Make Them Pay

The music box rested atop Harold's desk in his home office, a pretty little thing with exquisite wood carvings from the late Avant-Garde artist Amelia Danvers. A recent evaluation had determined its current market value was - at the very least - over three hundred thousand dollars. At the same time, it was considered a precious family heirloom that should never be sold away no matter the situation. If it ever came out that Harold was thinking of doing so to pay off gambling debts, he would be in dire trouble.

However, all things considered, he already was. Janusz "Six-Fingers" was known for leaving his enemies with none in the absence of payment. Sometimes, people lost other parts of their anatomy too and rumor had it that a select few had even misplaced their heads in bloody card boxes. Harold couldn't take that risk. While he had never been the sharpest tool in the box, he was still quite adamant about dying of old age and not in a dark alleyway on the eve of turning forty. The music box had to go so the money could flow. After he paid off what was owed (with interest, of course!), Janusz and he would finally part ways and never see their ugly faces again.

Harold poured a glass of Scotch and glanced at his smartphone. His contact was running late. If he didn't call soon, the window of opportunity to close the sale before anyone realized something was amiss would be gone. Cold sweat dripped from his wrinkled forehead as he mused on the oddities of the relic before him.

Old Aunt Margaret - rest in peace! - had once described it as "an instrument of evil" and Father Jeb, who was now closer to the grave than to claw his way out of it, mentioned a looming presence within it. Whether it was the ghost of Amelia Danvers herself or something else that words failed to properly describe was unknown. What was certain was that being in its presence for too long often induced an altered state of mind, something between extreme euphoria and fear. He could already feel the pull growing from the nether regions of his troubled psyche and yet, he would do the right thing and ignore it. If things worked out as planned, in a few hours, the box and the legends associated with it would be someone else's problem.

Harold laid down the glass and gasped as it shot forward across the table on its own to hit the allegedly cursed instrument and send it flying to the floor. His breath was suspended in the dreadful moment, for a broken item would also spell a broken life. He jumped out of his seat and saw that the box now laid open yet silent. No melody played from within its gears, but a column of billowing smoke was now rising towards the ceiling.

It was as black as the darkest night and so thick that it absorbed any light around it. Impressions of agonizing faces could be glimpsed all around, protruding and then retreating into the gloomy mass. The one exception took the shape of a cold and calculating female figure, emerging at will from its depths as if she were the force controlling them. It was definitely Amelia, and she had something to say,

"Alone, you're weak, but together, we'll be strong. Take my blessing and smile once again."

The column of smoke swirled above Harold's head who was too baffled to even utter a word. His half-open mouth was the perfect point of entrance for the demonic entity as it pillaged his waking thoughts one by one until nothing remotely human remained. Dropping to its knees, the meat sack grinned at its newfound power, staring vacantly into the checkered carpet. Janusz would surely love to have his own fingers served on a silver platter and should anyone dare to complain, they would all be turned into hosts as well.

Amelia Danvers had always been one step ahead of everyone in everything in life and now also in death, for the powerful souls always thrive. With a single piercing thought, she commanded her new puppet to rise,

"It's time to make them pay," she said, planting images of sharp knives in its skull. Once-Harold nodded and left the house in deathly silence. The phone call that arrived as he closed the door was already too late to stop the inevitable.

Pact of Darkness

Lauren stopped at the front door of her place to catch her breath, sweat dripping down her shoulders and thighs. The morning sprint had been harder than usual, because of yet another terrible sleep. The haunting dreams that tormented her all week kept on escalating, promising a confrontation of biblical proportions for her sanity. She wanted none of that. Why couldn't she be normal for a change?

As much as she hated to admit it, the answer lay in her bloodline. All the women in her family were witches, drawn to the supernatural arts like moths to a flame even if they tried to escape them. The power of her heritage was too strong. If she refused to heed the call while awake, she had to do it in her restless sleep.

Lauren sat on the cold floor and contemplated the quiet life of her neighbors. They were so lucky to not know what lurked in the shadows, waiting to claim their souls if they made one false move. Rare are the cases where true ignorance is bliss, but this was one of them.

Familiar faces passed by, smiling, but she paid no attention to them. Her mind was solely focused on the furious call coming from the depths of the earth. She was about to break free.

The futuristic sounds of a synth ringtone brought her phone to life, but the voice waiting for her on the other end of the call was another harbinger of doom.

"We need to talk," her coven sister, Danielle, said.

"Yeah, we do. How bad have the dreams been for you?"

"Too awful to put into words. The Seals have been broken."

"All of them?"

"No. Not yet at least. Camilla sensed one and Pauline another. If the other two suffer the same fate soon..."

"You don't need to remind me what will happen," Lauren banged the back of her head against the blue door, the image of a river of burning blood flooding her courtyard taking precedence over all other thoughts. She was dancing in it and enjoying it far too much.

"I don't want to submit to her," Danielle sobbed.

"Me neither, but what will you do if she demands your allegiance?"

"I won't let it come to that. If the choice is between her reign and my life, the answer is clear."

"Please don't do anything rash. We can still make it through this."

"Can we really, or are you just trying to lull yourself into a false sense of security?"

An excellent question, and one whose implications were also clear. The days of serving the Dark Mistress of the Underworld had faded from memory in the coven's ways, but the power of the old rituals still subsided. Could a Goddess be denied after taking corporeal shape again?

"I don't know what to say."

"Say you won't hang up no matter what you hear."

"Dani..."

"I mean it, Lauren."

"She'll just bring you back to life."

"No, that won't be me, just a husk. My soul will be long gone, free from her evil grasp."

"What about me?"

"If you're smart, you'll do the same. We can do it together to keep each other company until the very end."

"No. I'm not a coward. Call the others and let's meet to discuss a strategy."

"That's useless. I already made up my mind. If you're not with me, then the hell with you!"

"Dani, please..."

"Forget it, Lauren. This was a waste of time. I'll do it alone."

The call went silent, the inevitable demise sinking its sharp teeth into her soul. Lauren closed her eyes, tears rolling down her flustered cheeks, and the river of blood running stronger than ever. The pact of darkness would hold.

Somewhere deep beneath her feet, the third seal broke.

Perfect

All the monitors inside Zephyr's Industries Underground Lab 1 were flashing at the same time, the first sign that something was amiss. The noisy alarm came after, flooding all corridors in red and triggering everyone on the sub-floor into a panicking frenzy.

"What the hell is going on?" Dr. Reynolds came running into the Security Room, the first person to do so. She was the head of the project and the person everyone feared the most in the facilities and with good reason. The fair-skinned, dirty blonde had the face of an angel, but the personality of a horned devil, and anyone that got in her way was usually never seen again.

"We have a containment breach," Head of Security Malcolm Harris replied, right hand clutching his chest.

"Where?"

"The chambers beneath the lab. I can confirm that at least one of them is broken."

"What? But that's where we keep..."

"I know, Dr. We need to evacuate and burn the area to the ground immediately. Shall I give the order?"

"Are you out of your fucking mind? You will not burn two hundred million dollars' worth of research because of a breach that can be contained some other way. You may give the order to evacuate the surrounding laboratories, but nothing more. I'm heading there right now. Get me a team of twelve of your best men equipped with tranquilizer guns and once we're all inside, seal the bulkheads until this mess is sorted, understood?"

"Are you sure that is wise, Dr.? You know what those things can do!"

"You have your orders, soldier. Get a move on!"

"Yes, Dr."

Dr. Reynolds left the Security room and dashed to her private elevator. This was the last thing she needed, right on the eve of the quarterly evaluation. It wasn't just the funding on the line but also her job and reputation, two things she couldn't afford to lose.

Hired by Zephyr Industries two years prior, she had excelled in genetic manipulation far beyond what everyone thought possible. The first human-animal hybrids conceived in vitro had been grotesque aberrations, but necessary failures in the pursuit of perfection. Having finally worked through the issues that plagued her early work, she now had the opportunity to be acknowledged as a true genius as opposed to a mad one.

Dr. Reynolds reached the sub-floor and charged directly into the chamber's locations as the guards assigned to protect her and contain the menace arrived. Just as she had been told, one pod was shattered from the inside, its former resident standing in front of her.

It was a silver-skinned female with long curly hair of the same color, a cross between a normal woman and far too many animal traits to remember. Her eyes were fierce, sizing everyone gathering around her with undeniable ill-intent.

"Look at her!" Dr. Reynolds thought. "Why would you ever want to destroy perfection?"

The hybrid grinned, lidless pupils shining with recollection.

"Mother..." it hissed.

"Yes," the scientist nodded. "I'm your mother and you're absolutely majestic, my dear. You'll need to go back to sleep, though."

"No. No more sleep. You sleep! Yes... you sleep now."

"Dr.? What does she mean by that?"

"I don't..."

Suddenly, a choir of inhuman voices pierced her brain, like a siren's call amplified a thousand times or more. It rang deeper and deeper with her nervous central system, rendering the world blurry and indistinct. She screamed as her innards were turned into obedient jelly before her superior creation.

"How...?" she mumbled before collapsing into pure darkness. It was a question that would remain unanswered long after her personality was rewired into mindless submission. The last thing she saw as a free individual was the other five chambers opening up.

R & R

Tawnya stood by the bedroom mirror, trying out dresses for her best friend's birthday party when her boyfriend William knocked on the door. He had sweaty clothes and pleading eyes. His voice was like a soft murmur, almost as if he were afraid to talk to her.

"Honey, may I come in?"

"Sure," she replied looking at him with a green dress in one hand and a dark red in the other. "Which one do you like best?"

"They're both nice," he replied. "We need to talk."

"What is it this time?"

"I finished my chores for the day, and I was wondering if I could have a bit of R & R now," he produced a video game case, one of those ultra-difficult RPGs he loved so much.

"Hmmm... are you sure you took care of everything?"

"Yes, dear."

"Did you do the dishes?"

"Yes, dear."

"Did you take out the trash?"

"Yes, dear."

"Did you mow the lawn?"

"Yes, dear."

"Did you clean the garage?"

"Yes, dear."

"Hmmm," she undid her clothes to put on the green dress. "It seems you really did do everything you were told, but I have to ask: is playing that silly game more important than making me happy?"

"Of course not, but if we're through for the day, I thought I could..."

"Say no more," she raised her right back and pointed at her back. "Zip me up."

"Yes, dear."

William was in his early thirties and was quite the specimen of a man. He had piercing grey eyes, a chiseled jaw, and broad shoulders. He was often mistaken for a wrestler because of his imposing physique, but underneath all those muscles was a sweet teddy bear that was even sweeter when he was entranced. She had trained him well since they started dating, but clearly, that wasn't enough.

Tawnya paraded her tanned body in front of the mirror and smiled. The choice was made.

"Okay," she said. "You can relax now."

"Seriously?" his eyes lit up. "Thank you."

"On one condition..." she placed a solitary finger on his slightly wet lips.

"What is it?"

"You let me take care of everything for you."

"That's unexpected."

"You work so hard to pamper me that I want to do the same for you for a change. Is that okay?"

"Anything you say, dear."

"Good. Give me the game and go sit on the couch. I'll be right there with you."

"Thank you."

William exited the bedroom, feeling happier than ever. Despite everything she put him through, she loved him and that made him the luckiest man in the world. He descended the stairs into the living room and stretched on the leather sofa.

Tawnya came to him less than five minutes later with a tray of salty snacks and a cold drink. She turned on the TV and said,

"There you go, dear. Enjoy."

The screen illuminated with golden light, but instead of the game's title screen what awaited him was a mesmerizing swirl and a string of white words urging him to relax.

"Wait, this isn't..." he muttered.

"This is exactly what you need. Rest, dear. Fix your eyes on the entrancing pattern and go down for me again."

"I... yes, dear," William droned, mind going blank. He had forgotten this was how things always played out whenever she did something nice for him, but the memories were never gone for long.

"Good boy. We'll do one hour today to reinforce your programming. When you're done, go paint the fence outside and clean the pool. I'll be waiting."

William exhaled all resistance in a single breath, drooping eyes following the rest of his body into a trance. Rest and recreation? More like "rinse and repeat". The slave in him had a lot of work ahead.

Relaxing Weekend

"Stupid mosquitoes!" Willa grumbled as she swatted another blood-sucking insect from her right arm.

"Why are you so jumpy?" Aiko asked, her delicate oriental features bathed by the pale moonlight and the fire between them.

"Because I didn't want to come camping! I can't believe you persuaded me into this. I hate this!"

The two of them sat in the wilderness, three hundred miles away from the bustling metropolis that demanded their sweat and tears every day and offered little solace. Stress had become so indelibly stamped in Aiko's daily routine that she had decided the time was right for a peaceful retreat. One would expect the love of her life to agree, and yet she was miserable.

"Well, I love it. It's so peaceful and serene around here."

"Tell that to these flying bitches that won't leave me alone."

"Calm down, please. It's not that bad."

"I disagree. Do we really need to stay here all weekend?"

"I would prefer if we did. Are you in such a hurry to go back to the frenzy?"

"At least, it's predictable," Willa sighed. "It's not a pretty routine, but it has its advantages."

"I see none at the moment. Perhaps there's something I can do to soften the blow."

"Hmmm... What do you have in mind?"

"To put yours to sleep," Aiko smiled in that enigmatic way only she could do. Willa knew the power it held all too well for it had contributed to the blooming of their misunderstood relationship. Neither of their families approved of the choice, their minds clouded by prejudice and hate, but no storm had ever come between them and, despite some rough moments here and there, the situation was unlikely to change.

"Hypnosis again? Do you still enjoy it that much?"

"Don't you?"

"Well, it is quite the experience..." Willa agreed, reminiscing about all the times she had been compelled to follow her lead. In fact, she was almost certain that the whole camping idea had been triggered by something similar but couldn't pinpoint when or how.

"And good experiences are those you wish to repeat time and time again..."

"But let's not forget that too much repetition of the same thing can make it stale or sour..."

"That is true when you're talking about physical things you can touch, but that's not what hypnosis is, is it? It is a ride of the mind, an intangible feeling that draws you in like the embers of a flame. There's a reason so many people find it easy to let go of their worries next to a fire, for its warmth and gentle flickers lull them gently, like a mother rocking her baby child into a peaceful slumber."

"I'm not a baby, Aiko."

"Of course, you are. You're my baby, my everything, and you'll always be that. You accept this as I do, and the fire too. Looking through it to find me makes your eyes feel so heavy... so sleepy... completely at ease, relaxed, and content. The flames burn more than the logs that feed them. They also snuff out the things you wish gone more than everything."

"Which are...?"

"The ability to think anything other than my words, hearing my thoughts in your head, and doing as you're told to go deeper... deeper... and deeper."

"You don't know everything about me," Willa moaned, legs slightly apart.

"I know enough to make you drop *snap*, again *snap* and again *snap*, deeper *snap* and deeper *snap*, swept by the flame, burning for me."

Willa's head slumped forward, though she remained seated on the warm mattress. Aiko was right, and the burning light agreed. The full moon continued to watch over the two lovers in silent adoration until only a faint column of smoke spiraled into the sky. Stress was no more, but the bliss of peaceful trance was forever.

Sensation Play

Janet touched Frankie's right leg and asked,

"How does this feel?"

"Cold," her girlfriend replied. "Oh, fuck, it's so cold!"

Janet noted her reaction and placed another finger on the same spot,

"How about now?"

"Hot! Oh, my God, it burns! It burns! Stop!"

"Shhh... easy now," Janet removed her fingers and lulled her favorite person in the world back to deep hypnotic sleep. "It's okay, sweetie. Everything is fine. Take a deep breath and relax. Do you trust me?"

"Yes," came the immediate response. Frankie had a lot of flaws but failing to trust the woman she loved was not one of them. Her breathing slowed down, heart rate becoming so silent one could easily think she had died on the spot. It was her first time going under and as expected, her responses were somewhat erratic. Sometimes, it was too much to handle, but it was something they could fix.

"Good. Focus on my voice and my voice alone. Everything you've experienced so far was not real. It's all on your mind. There's no ice and no fire on your leg. It only feels like that because you're imagining it to be true, so clear your head and put those sensations away. My voice will tell you what to do and what to feel. Trust my voice and go a little deeper this time in three, two, one..."

Frankie's head bobbed as if she were a spring doll, muscles loosening with Janet's suggestions. If everything was just in her head, then who was to say that she wasn't fantasizing about being hypnotized, too? Her girlfriend's voice became increasingly more distant, an echo underwater muffled by the currents of her stray thoughts.

"How deep are you now?" Janet asked.

"At the very bottom," Frankie replied. In her mind's eye, she pictured a never-ending ocean filled with what appeared to be remnants of great civilizations the world had learned to forget. She sat on the ocean floor, grains of golden sand glistening through her wrinkled fingers. The longer she stayed there, breathing in the salted water, the more she forgot who she was.

"You can always go deeper, but for now stay there. Think of nothing else except the fact that you're safe. You're always safe when you're locked in my voice. There's no pain in this world, nothing can hurt you unless you allow it to. There's only my voice. Repeat it now, dear."

"There's only your voice."

"Yes, excellent! And my voice is now telling you will not feel a thing. You will feel nothing that comes next. Keep relaxing for me,"

Janet reached for an ice cube and rubbed it on her legs, moving dangerously close to her tight slit, but Frankie remained perfectly still, unbothered by the cold wetness she could no longer notice.

"What am I doing now?" Frankie asked.

"Nothing."

"That's right, nothing is happening. You can block out all sensations by simply believing it so, but if you focus on the opposite for just one second..."

Frankie's legs started shivering, enveloped by a cold Arctic wind. Her lips immediately turned blue.

"Hmmm... not again! It's freezing... ah!"

"Shhh, no it's not," Janet reassured her. "Nothing is happening, and nothing ever will. Do you want to be cold?"

"No."

"Do you want to be warm?"

"No."

"What do you want, then?"

"To feel your fingers inside my pussy," Frankie moaned.

"We don't need hypnosis for that, but I'm happy to oblige. Open your legs for me, my love."

Frankie bit her lower lip, overwhelmed by anticipatory bliss. The sensation of her control would only grow more intense as time went by.

The Great Fire of Elsworth

The Avery Triplets were Elsworth's most kept secret, forces of nature recently turned twenty-two that paraded their exotic looks around the city and surrounding neighborhoods in latex mini-skirts, conquering everything in their path. Alone, they were already almost impossible to resist, but when they got together, the power they unleashed brought even the strongest of minds to heel.

Her names were Alana, Brenda, and Claudia, the ABC of mesmerizing seduction, witches born of witches that did what other witches dared not. They walked out and about, showing off their powers without a care in the world. If any man and woman on Elsworth tried to deny their superiority, they would end up as groveling boot slaves, or worse, be turned into something unnatural. That ten-legged bug crawling around the main street? Yes, it used to be a normal person just like you and me.

I met the sisters on the very first day I moved to Elsworth, twelve years ago. Even at a tender age, they already exhibited malevolent traits that couldn't be contained though they waited for their coming-of-age ceremony to let them run wild. It was on that dreadful night they claimed me as their own. I love them as much as I despise them, for I know the thoughts in my head are the by-product of their dark spells. This is not a tale I wish to write, but I will, for I'm compelled by their luscious presence.

It was the day after St. Patrick's and Elsworth had woken up covered in green. Thick vines could be seen everywhere from the hardware store on the edge of the city to the Mayor's office in the center. Cars and stray people had been swallowed by them too, with only faint traces of their past presence visible under the morning sky. My words will never do justice to the horrors I've seen, so forgive them in advance.

They were having breakfast outside. I was trapped inside the magical cage they built for me in their garden, listening to their plans for the day, and this is what came to be,

"I thought green was the way to go, but don't you girls think we overdid it?" Alana asked.

"Yeah," Brenda said. "It's too much green. It really doesn't match the color of my outfit," she pointed at her red top and matching skirt.

"I'm with you two, so let's do something about it," Claudia concurred. "How about we burn them all at the same time? That way we can get yellow, orange, red, and the blackness of the smoke enveloping everything."

"I love it!" Alana exclaimed. "Shall we do it right away?"

"Let me finish my food first," Brenda giggled. "You know magic and an empty stomach don't go hand in hand."

"Agreed. Here, mutt," Claudia threw a small piece of apple pie my way. "Enjoy it while you can."

I hate to admit I ate it off the wet grass, but I was hungry too. No more pieces were handed out and the hole in my belly was never closed. Even if it had, my appetite would have to shit afterward, anyway.

The Avery Triplets stood up from their seats and joined hands to produce the greatest blaze known to mankind. The flames were so intense they could be seen from outer space, something which I never thought possible. They ravaged everything mercilessly, turning green hope into dead ash while their other thralls applauded their audacity, including my parents. History will never write that The Great Fire of Elsworth was caused by supernatural powers, but the truth is clear. I acknowledge it, and now so do you.

Do not, under any circumstance, visit this place, because they're still around and they can't enough of having more slaves to use and abuse. For now, they're still content with terrorizing what they already know, though I fear for the day they decide it's time to take a trip around the world. If you ever see three golden-haired women wearing latex skirts coming your way, do the right thing and run.

The Woman You See

Every night, just before you go to bed, you see her, sometimes standing next to you, and other times in the reflection of the nearest mirror. You see her wearing leather, latex, or PVC, tapping the floor with six-inch heels, or touching the soles of her thigh-high boots while staring at you. You don't know for sure who she is and yet it's as if she's been a part of your life forever. This woman never speaks, but you can describe her voice perfectly. It is the embodiment of Power, raining down on you from the heavens. Even if you look away, she's always there, waiting. You can hear her breathing behind you right now.

So, who is she? The answer will vary depending on who you ask. A therapist might say she's an idealized version of your subconscious desires for dominance and submission. A specialist in the occult will say it's a ghost with unfinished business that has latched on to you for some obscure reason, and a hypnodomme will tell you that it's you, or rather who you desperately wish to be as she pulls the strings of your persona in whatever way it makes her happy. There's no resisting her charms, and she knows it. Do you?

Now, I know you don't want to believe this possibility at all, but if you think about it for more than a few seconds, you realize it makes perfect sense. Here you are, eyes glued on the screen, reading about femdom hypnosis and mind control. After a while, it's only natural that these ideas rub off on you and that fetishes you never wanted to explore become something you can't stop thinking about. Brainwashing a mind starts with these innuendos, small things are hidden in plain view that then grow into something beyond your control. These seeds are everywhere, especially in stories, for what better way to reconstruct the truth than through a work of fiction? Yes, it is possible, and now you're thinking the same thing. See how easy that is?

And now, you're confused. The inner gears of your brain are telling you that something like this can happen, then where does it stop? What else have you been indoctrinated into without realizing it, and how will you respond to the next triggers as they come along? Will you try to stay awake, noticing the ruse through and through, or will you close your eyes, dream a little, and pretend you've merely imagined it all? It's not an easy choice, or is it? Do you even have the power to choose anything in your life anymore? Hmm...

Yes, think about this. Let this idea bloom behind your eyelids. It will be your new addiction and your new uncontrolled obsession. The more you try to resist being mind-controlled the more you'll be under the influence of it. And when you started believing that you broke free is when its grip on you will be the strongest.

The woman you see will never go away, so do the right thing and embrace the madness, dear. It is your past, your present, and your future. Deeper now.

Unfinished Business

Every living soul in the peaceful village of Cleas, Ireland, had heard at least one story about Marie Winterbottom, the spirit said to dwell in the dusty halls of forgotten Creek Manor. The details of the accounts varied depending on the person telling them and whatever point they were trying to get across. Some tales were sad, others downright bloody but, most of the time, they landed somewhere in the middle. Marie was either a scorned lover, a grieving mother, or a frenzied widow. It mattered not as long as one particular idea shone through. She had unfinished business on the mortal plane of existence, and that's why she couldn't leave.

With time, the people of the village had learned to ignore the Manor completely and only ever mentioned Marie in passing to tourists or other passersby. Jim Hayes hadn't gone there for the sights but to tell a tale of his own in the form of an article about rural Ireland and its curiosities. Creek Manor fitted the profile and so did he, for he had been blessed with a gift few others possessed. He could see ghosts, whether they wanted to be seen or not, or no longer had the power to manifest themselves properly.

On the last Saturday of March, under the light of a blue moon, he entered the derelict house and saw her, standing by a window, gazing outside at a distant point on the horizon. She still had the complexion of an early twenties woman despite being dead for over eighty years. Her hair was blonde and short, her physique small and understated. She possessed none of the ridiculous attributes that made men go crazy, but only a simple, classic, and serene beauty that said she could do no harm.

"Hello," Jim said, notebook and camera in hand.

"You can see me?" the ghost gasped when she realized she wasn't alone.

"As clear as day. I heard a lot about you over the years, Marie. It's a pleasure to finally meet you."

"And you are..."

"My name is Jim Hayes, and I'm a reporter for..."

"Ah, a reporter..." she interrupted him dismissively. "Another bloodsucking vampire wanting to feast on my misery... Please go away if that's what you're here for. I'm not interested."

"I wish to feast on nothing, merely learn. You've become a legend, but all legends have some truth in them. Yours fascinates me."

"Why?"

"Because of my connections to the spirit world. From an early age, I realized I could see things others couldn't, and that has given me a greater understanding of reality itself. You're hurt and trapped in here. Perhaps I can help you escape this torment."

"You want to send me into the light, Mr. Reporter?"

"I want you to be free as everyone deserves to be, alive or not. Why are you stuck? Do you know?"

"Yes, I do," Marie sighed. "Something was stolen from me, something so precious that without it, my soul can't move on in either direction. I need it back."

"What is this precious heirloom?"

"A locket. I wore it from the day I was born to the day I died. It was taken from my cold body and buried in the woods past this house. I know where it is because I can feel its presence, but I can't go out and get it. Would you retrieve it for me?"

"If that's what it takes to solve your issues, yes. Tell me where it is, and I'll go find it."

"Really?"

"Yes."

"Past the first row of willows, slightly turned to the east, there's a marker with a red stone. Fifty paces north from there, you'll find an old animal burial ground. My locket is there, right where the road ends. Please... if you're serious, bring it to me as quickly as possible."

"I'm already on my way."

Jim left the manor and followed the directions given without a hassle. Everything was just as she had described, proof of her psychic connection to the missing object. The locket was a simple silver trinket, but it had a lot of history attached to it. A single drop of blood lay crystallized in the place where a picture was supposed to be.

Silently, the reporter negotiated a path back to the manor and proudly exhibited the item in his right hand. Marie was immediately ecstatic.

"You did it! I spent years trying to convince others to get it for me only to be forgotten here and then you come out of nowhere and fix everything. This is amazing!"

"I'm glad. Are you ready to leave now?"

"I have a better idea," she smirked. "Kneel."

Jim frowned at first, but his knees complied anyway, sinking on the old wooden floors with a thud. The object felt warm in his hand, irradiating otherworldly energies too powerful to be resisted.

"Good boy. Now, put the locket around your neck," Marie commanded.

Once again, the confused man obeyed, her presence becoming stronger in his psyche.

"Wonderful," she declared. "We are now connected by that drop of blood; our energies are intertwined. The longer you wear this trinket the less you'll be able to fight my control. You're no longer a reporter, you're my slave. Say it."

"I'm your slave, Marie," he replied.

"Good slave. Now, I can leave. Your body serves as an anchor tethering me to the outside world and wherever your body goes, so can I. Many people wronged me before my passing and even though they're no longer alive, vengeance is a generational affair. We're going to visit those that remain. You have a car, right?"

"Yes, Marie."

"Mistress Marie, slave. Get up and take me to your vehicle. Our little road trip begins now."

Jim's puppet body followed her lead, independent thoughts fading one by one. Mistress Marie was in charge now, and retribution would be painful for everyone involved.

About the stories in this volume

The twelve pieces of flash fiction included in this book were written between March 4th, 2022, and March 18th, 2022, and first published on my Patreon page – https://www.patreon.com/sbspellbound - as part of the *Flash Fiction Friday* feature. Every Friday, I publish 3/4 new pieces of content which, after a while, are compiled to create the titles in this ongoing series. If you like this sort of content and wish to see more, please consider supporting my creativity. The complete information about the tales is listed below:

- **Afraid of Himself** - Andrew thinks about doing impossible things to please the woman that controls his mind.
  (This piece was first published on the post "Flash Fiction Friday 2022 – Week 11", on March 18th, 2022 - https://www.patreon.com/posts/63966056)
- **Glory to Harukka!** - Yasmin is being reprogrammed to serve a higher power inside the law firm she works for.
  (This piece was first published on the post "Flash Fiction Friday 2022 – Week 11", on March 18th, 2022 - https://www.patreon.com/posts/63966056)
- **It's My Turn Again** - Alan doesn't understand how Melissa became such a good chess player overnight. What's her secret?

(This piece was first published on the post "Flash Fiction Friday 2022 – Week 9", on March 4th, 2022 - https://www.patreon.com/posts/63376200)

- **Make Them Pay** - Harold wants to sell a music box to pay off gambling debts, but the relic has other plans.
(This piece was first published on the post "Flash Fiction Friday 2022 – Week 9", on March 4th, 2022 - https://www.patreon.com/posts/63376200)
- **Pact of Darkness** - Lauren realizes something is amiss in the world and that her bloodline has something to do with it.
(This piece was first published on the post "Flash Fiction Friday 2022 – Week 9", on March 4th, 2022 - https://www.patreon.com/posts/63376200)
- **Perfect** - A genetically-engineered hybrid escapes its confinement at an underground private laboratory.
(This piece was first published on the post "Flash Fiction Friday 2022 – Week 10", on March 11th, 2022 - https://www.patreon.com/posts/63684318)
- **R & R** - William asks for a break after working all day, but his girlfriend has something else in mind.
(This piece was first published on the post "Flash Fiction Friday 2022 – Week 10", on March 11th, 2022 - https://www.patreon.com/posts/63684318)
- **Relaxing Weekend** - Willa and Aiko go camping to escape the stress of the big city and have some fun.

(This piece was first published on the post "Flash Fiction Friday 2022 – Week 9", on March 4th, 2022 - https://www.patreon.com/posts/63376200)

- **Sensation Play** - Janet teaches Frankie how to feel the things she wants her to while in trance.
(This piece was first published on the post "Flash Fiction Friday 2022 – Week 10", on March 11th, 2022 - https://www.patreon.com/posts/63684318)

- **The Great Fire of Elsworth** - A man recalls a terrible event that took place in a small American city, but what caused it?
(This piece was first published on the post "Flash Fiction Friday 2022 – Week 11", on March 18th, 2022 - https://www.patreon.com/posts/63966056)

- **The Woman You See** - An experimental piece about thoughts, beliefs, and an obsession you can't explain.
(This piece was first published on the post "Flash Fiction Friday 2022 – Week 10", on March 11th, 2022 - https://www.patreon.com/posts/63684318)

- **Unfinished Business** - Jim tries to help Marie's spirit to move on and find her peace in the afterlife.
(This piece was first published on the post "Flash Fiction Friday 2022 – Week 11", on March 18th, 2022 - https://www.patreon.com/posts/63966056)

About the author

S.B., Simple Being, middle name Creative. Writer and artist with a penchant for themes of Femdom Hypnosis and Mind Control. His thoughts are his own except when they're not.

Besides indulging himself in kinky delights, he loves his furry family of two (dogs), sci-fi and horror stories, and puns galore. He's also been writing a piece of erotic micro-fiction every single day since January 1st, 2016 and has no intention of stopping anytime soon.

Find out more and keep up with his latest extravaganzas by visiting and supporting his personal website, Spell… B-O-U-N-D.